E
ER I   Erickson, Phoebe   c1

          Slip, the story of a
          little fox

Child Coll

DATE			

© THE BAKER & TAYLOR CO.

SLIP

The Story of a Little Fox

Story and Pictures by
Phoebe Erickson

CHILDRENS PRESS, CHICAGO

To Pat and Lotta

Library of Congress Catalog Card Number: 48-4154

Four little foxes were born in the early spring. They lived in a den, deep under the ground. For a few weeks they spent most of their time sleeping. Then one day Mother Fox carried them, one at a time, up into the light.

Soon they were rolling and tumbling in the leaves, chasing their tails, and playing endless games.

One day Mother Fox said, "Now, my children, you must learn to be clever little foxes. When you are clever enough, you can hunt with your father."

A catbird was watching them. "Now if you could teach them to fly," he said.

"I could teach you a trick or two," said Mother Fox, and she went on with the lesson.

The little foxes learned quickly. Except Slip. He was curious about other things.

One night a great white moon rose over the ridge. Higher and higher it climbed, until its light flooded the valley. The shadows in the little wood became black, but here and there a silvery patch of light danced through the trees.

Slip, the little red fox, sat under a fiddle fern watching it.

"What's that, Mother?" he asked, pointing his nose toward the sky.

"Just the moon," answered Mother. "Stay in the shadows and keep your wits about you."

"Where is the moon going?"

"It goes a long way and drops into the Bears' Big Wood."

Slip shivered, then went into the den.

Late that same night Father Fox came home carrying a fat hen. The little ones were asleep in the den, their bushy tails wrapped over their heads.

"What a time I had, getting that hen home," Father Fox said. "I ran miles before I threw Farmer McGarry's dog off my trail by running on a rail fence. He went past me, but he had his nose to the ground, so he didn't see me."

"You are a very clever fellow!" said Mother Fox.
"How are the little ones coming along?"

"They're learning. All but the smallest one."

"Humph!" grunted Father. "Why, when I was his age
. . . " He glanced over his shoulder, and gave a low growl.

Where was that hen he had brought home? He crept
quietly around the thicket. And there was Slip, eating
the hen.

"Well I never," exclaimed Mother Fox.

"Humph!" said Father stalking off to bed. "He's
learning."

The morning sun peeped into the thicket. It sparkled and danced on the dew drops. The sleeping buds of the flowers opened wide.

The four little foxes blinked in the brilliance of the morning. Slip felt fine this morning. Any day now he would be going hunting with his father.

"Good morning, good morning," cawed a crow.

"Good morning, yourself," answered the catbird. "Can you imagine such a thing?" he said, coming down to a low branch. "That crow thinks he can sing. Now if you want to hear real singing, listen to this."

He perked up his tail and began: "Cheer-up, cheer-up, tou-ee, tou-ee, chip, chip, chip, do-do de-dee, pee-wee, pee-wee, whip-poor-will, whip-poor-will, meow, m-e-o-w . . ."

The little foxes looked at him with admiration. Here was a catbird singing the songs of all the birds and imitating a cat, too.

"I know more songs. Do you want to hear them?"

"Quiet!" barked Father Fox. "What with dogs and birds, there is no peace anywhere." He curled himself up on a rock and went back to sleep.

"I think I'll be going along," said the catbird. Then he added quietly to Slip, "Why don't you just slip off and show them how clever you are?"

Slip thought that was a good idea. He began to wander along the brook, curious about everything.

He saw a boy sitting on a rock, fishing. Slip sat down behind some bushes to watch him. Suddenly a fish seemed to leap out of the water. The boy took it off the hook, put a string through its gills, and tossed it into the bushes.

"This is too easy," thought Slip as he quietly picked up the fish and started home. "Surely I am a clever fellow. And I have a fish to prove it."

He laid the fish triumphantly at his father's feet.

"How nice," said Father. "A fish for my breakfast."

"Am I clever enough to hunt with you?"

Father Fox laughed. He saw the string through the gills. "Anyone can catch a fish that is on dry land. You can't fool me!"

All the little foxes laughed at Slip.

Slip wandered off again. Without knowing where he was going, he passed through Mr. McGarry's meadow. Suddenly he stopped and his fur bristled. He peeked cautiously through the tall grass and saw a wolf, gnawing at something.

Slip crept quietly away. It was best to leave his kind alone.

But before he got out of the open meadow, the farmer's dog was after him. Slip didn't know which way to go.

He thought of the brook, but it was too far.

He looked for the rail fence, but the dog was between him and the fence.

The wolf! Slip whirled suddenly and ran straight at him. The wolf was so surprised to see a fox coming right at him that he forgot to run. Fox and dog were almost upon him. Then with a snarl, the wolf dashed off, but the dog was after him.

Slip was safe now. "My, my, but I'm a clever fellow," he thought. And grinning to himself he trotted toward the den.

"Wherever have you been?" asked Mother **Fox**.

"Oh, I've just been outwitting the dog and the wolf." Then he told his mother all about it.

"Well, you are surely clever enough to go hunting with Father Fox. You just run along and find him."

"Where, where?"

"Today he has gone to the Bears' Big Wood."

"The—Bears' Big Wood?" Slip swallowed the fright lump in his throat. Then Slip remembered that he was a very clever fellow. He bristled the hairs along his neck to make himself feel brave — and off he went.

Slip followed the stream toward the Bears' Big Wood. The stream became wider. It tumbled over great rocks and made a roaring sound. Huge dark trees grew along its banks. Slip felt the quiet strangeness of the place.

A doe and her two fawns came down to the stream to drink.

"Good evening, Mother Deer," said Slip in a friendly voice.

The doe looked up, startled, but when she saw who it was she replied, "Good evening, little fox." The fawns stared at him with big eyes. "What brings you to the Bears' Big Wood?"

"I am looking for Father Fox."

"We have not seen him."

Slip trotted on along the stream.

SPLASH! Something hit the water. Slip looked around. Down the steep bank came an otter, its front feet folded under it. PLOP! Into the pool it went. Soon there were many of them, running up the bank and sliding down again. Slip wished he could play with them. But he went on.

At last, too tired to go another step, Slip curled up on a log and went to sleep.

He was wakened by heavy footsteps coming through the bushes. A gray mist rose from the river and here and there a bird twittered. Slip lay very still.

Soon Mother Black Bear passed near him. Behind her the little cubs were rolling and tumbling over each other through the underbrush.

Mother Bear gave one a cuff with her paw and sent them up a tree to keep them out of mischief.

"Oh, I wish I could play with them," said Slip.

"You do, do you?" growled a deep voice, and Father Bear lumbered out of the bushes. "You foxes are full of tricks."

Father Bear knocked the top off an old rotted stump with one swat of his big paw.

"What delicious ants," said Mother Bear, licking them off her paws.

Father Bear was not looking at the ants. He was looking at Slip.

"Ah—er—" began Slip. He bristled the hair along his neck and tried to think like a fox. "You are a big fellow, aren't you?"

"Of course," rumbled the bear. He stood up on his hind feet to show how big he was.

"L-l-let's see how f-f-far you can reach up that t-t-tree," stammered Slip.

The bear lumbered toward a claw-marked pine.

Slip darted off through the brush and rocks. From a safe distance, he watched Father Bear huffing and puffing and clawing the tree.

Slip trotted on along the stream, tired and hungry. The air carried a strange whiff of danger.

Slip settled down behind a log to look around. Caution, he thought, is an important part of being clever.

An opossum climbed to the safety of a tree branch with her babies on her back.

Slip saw the doe and her fawns come quietly out of the wood to drink.

The wolf limped down to the river to bathe his paws.

The doe lifted her head and saw that the wolf could not hurt a mouse. She went on drinking.

The wind still carried the strange smell of danger to Slip. His sharp eyes studied every inch of the wood along the river.

And then he saw it! A soft, light ball crouched on the branch of a tree. The moon! The moon had dropped into the Bears' Big Wood. But it looked more like Farmer McGarry's cat — only bigger, much bigger. And it had eyes that followed every movement of the fawns.

The opossum began to chatter. "We are all in danger with that lynx in the tree."

"Lynx?" gulped Slip.

"Well, DO something!"

"Me?" Slip bristled the hair along his neck and settled down a little deeper behind his log.

Then with just one eye above the log he saw something that made his heart turn over.

Father Fox was coming along the stream on his way home. He held his head high and lifted his feet in his dapper manner.

He had not yet caught the danger smell, and in a minute he would be directly under the branch that held the big cat.

Slip leaped over his log and streaked along the river like a red ball of noise and fury. He did not have time to think like a fox. "Yap—yap—yap, run, run!" he barked.

The doe and the fawns wheeled into the protection of the wood. Birds began to scold and chatter. Father Fox turned and ran with Slip. They crossed and recrossed the stream to break their trail.

Finally Father Fox stopped to rest.

"What is all this nonsense?" he growled. "Are you up to one of your tricks?"

The catbird settled down on a low branch and began: "Cheer-up, cheer-up, tou-ee, chip, chip, meow."

"Quiet!" growled Father Fox. "What with little yapping foxes and birds there is no peace around here."

"There is no danger either, thanks to Slip," said the catbird.

"What's that?" asked Father Fox.

"There was a lynx in the tree, that's what," said the catbird. "Slip warned the fawns and ran you out of danger."

"You did that?" Father Fox sat down and looked at Slip.

Slip looked at the ground. "I'm not very clever. I couldn't even think like a fox. I just ran and yapped."

"That is good enough for me. Come along. You can teach the other little foxes a thing or two."

When they reached home, Slip was the center of attention. The little foxes looked at him with admiration. Mother Fox looked at him with pride, and Father Fox looked at him as though he were seeing him for the first time. Such a clever little fellow, and right in his own family!

That night a great white moon rose over the ridge. Higher and higher it climbed, until its light flooded the valley. The shadows in the little wood became black, but here and there a silvery patch of light danced through the trees.

Slip, the little red fox, sat under a fiddle fern watching it.